Hi, Jamie!
   Guess what? I just got
a raise in my allowance!
See you at school.
   Anna

"Jamie, I've got a surprise for you," my mom
tells me.

I look up. "A bigger allowance?"

She laughs. "Even better. Grandpa Gus is coming!"

"Hooray!" I yell.

We only get to see Grandpa Gus during vacation. He doesn't visit much, because he's so busy on his farm.

Grandpa Gus is the best. He taught me how to ride a two-wheeler and how to whistle with a blade of grass. We even made our own strawberry jam. I got to help him pick the berries, too.

CHECK IT OUT!

by Nan Walker
illustrated by Blanche Sims

Kane Press, Inc.
New York

To the nicest editors ever—N.W. and B.S.
To Babe and Bernie Fuchs—Love, Blanche

Text copyright © 2006 by Nan Walker.
Illustrations copyright © 2006 by Blanche Sims.

Library of Congress Cataloging-in-Publication Data

Walker, Nan.
    Check it out! / by Nan Walker ; illustrated by Blanche Sims.
        p. cm. — (Social studies connects)
    "History - Grades: 1-3."
    Summary: Jamie finds it difficult to believe Grandpa Gus's stories about how much allowance he
got and the amount of television he watched as a child, until she begins to do some research into
the past.
    ISBN 1-57565-166-1 (alk. paper)
    [1. History—Fiction. 2. Grandfathers—Fiction.] I. Sims, Blanche, ill. II. Title. III. Series.
    PZ7.W153643Che 2006
    [Fic]—dc22
                                                    2005021198

10 9 8 7 6 5 4 3 2 1

First published in the United States of America in 2006 by Kane Press, Inc.
Printed in Hong Kong.

Social Studies Connects is a trademark of Kane Press, Inc.

Book Design: Edward Miller

www.kanepress.com

The doorbell rings, and I race downstairs. "Hey, Grandpa!"

He gives me a big hug and a gigantic stuffed giraffe. "How is my best girl?" he asks. "Are they treating you right?"

Grandpa Gus is just joking around. But he gives me an idea.

After lunch I ask Mom and Dad for a raise in my
allowance. "Anna gets fifty cents more than I do.
And Ricky gets a dollar more."

Grandpa's eyebrows shoot up. "A dollar more!"

My plan is working! I *knew* he'd take my side.

"When I was your age," Grandpa tells me, "I cleaned the henhouse, milked the cow, and slopped the hogs. And do you know how much I earned?"

I shake my head.

"Twenty-five cents!" He chuckles. "One shiny quarter. I was glad to have it, too."

My dad looks at me. "Maybe we should get a hog for you to slop."

Not funny.

A **source** is a person, place, or thing that gives you information. You can learn about the past by studying historical sources—from the pyramids to last year's newspapers!

So much for my brilliant plan.

I flip on the TV. *Laugh Track* is just starting. That should cheer me up.

Grandpa walks by. "Watching TV in the middle of the afternoon?" he asks. "When I was your age, we never turned the set on in the daytime. We ran around outside getting fresh air."

Mom gives me a look.

Click! Off goes the TV,
and out I go.

Hmmph. I don't want to hear anything else
about when Grandpa was my age. I'm starting to
think he's making it all up.

Twenty-five cents a week allowance? Kids who
would rather get fresh air than watch TV?

Yeah, right!

After dinner Dad makes hot chocolate, and we sit around and talk. Grandpa Gus is surprised that I have my own computer.

"Lots of kids do," I tell him. "My friend Anna just got a new one for her birthday."

He shakes his head. "When I was your age, a kid was lucky to have a *radio.*"

People are great sources of information. They can tell stories to give you an idea of what life was like in their time.

Here we go again. I'd better change the subject before Mom and Dad decide I don't need my own computer.

"Hey, look!" I point out the window. "It's snowing. Maybe we won't have school tomorrow."

Grandpa gets a gleam in his eye. "Aw, this isn't real snow," he says. "When I was a kid, the snow came down so hard it buried houses right up to the rooftops. Now, *that* was snow!"

Guess what? No snow day.

Grandpa Gus even has the weather on his side.

I trudge through the snow to pick up Ricky at his grandma's house. We always walk to school together.

"Unbelievable," I grumble as I wait for Ricky
to finish breakfast. "Absolutely unbelievable."

"What is?" he asks.

I tell him about Grandpa Gus and all his
stories. "Snow up to the rooftops," I say. "Right.
Grandpa's pretty old, but I don't think he was
around during the Ice Age."

Oops. Ricky's grandma, Mrs. Vega, hears me. "Snow up to the rooftops?" she asks. "You must mean the Great Blizzard of '49!"

"It really snowed that much?" I gasp.

"Biggest storm in history," she tells us, "and no one saw it coming. The weather report that morning said there might be flurries."

One way to look for the real facts is to check out primary sources. A **primary source** is first-hand information told or written by someone who actually lived through an event.

Someone who lived through the Blizzard of 1949 would be a primary source. So would an article, letter, or journal entry he or she wrote. Other primary sources include photos, invitations, tickets, ads, speeches—even school report cards!

Mrs. Vega shows us an old scrapbook. "Here I am, building a snowman—right out of my bedroom window!"

"That's amazing, Grandma!" Ricky says.

"Haven't you ever seen the marker on the town hall?" she asks. "They put it up to show how deep the snow was."

Ricky and I flip through the scrapbook.
"Look at that car!" he says.
"Check out the clothes!" I say.
"Take a look at the clock," says Mrs. Vega.
Clock? There's no clock in these photos.
Yikes! She means look at the time. We're going
to be late!

"Why don't you come back with Ricky after school?" Mrs. Vega suggests. "I have lots of childhood goodies in the attic."

It's fun to compare old photographs with new ones to see how things have changed over time.

17

GREAT BLIZZARD OF 1949
On February 10, the snow
reached this line

"It snowed a lot." —Mayor Dudley

Buildings can be good
sources of information.
So can monuments,
statues, and gravestones.

When we reach the town hall, I slow down
long enough to look for the snow marker. Sure
enough, there it is.

So maybe Grandpa Gus's story about the snow
was true. But what about his other stories?

I decide to check them out.

At library time, Ricky and I head straight for the history shelves.

We find tons of books. I never knew there was so much stuff about the old days.

A library is a great place for detective work about the past. You can find all kinds of information there. Try museums, too!

Wow! Things really *were* different when Grandpa Gus was my age. There were only forty-eight states! There were no cell phones, no microwaves, no video games, and no DVDs.

"Can you believe this?" I say. "When you went to buy shoes, you could x-ray your own feet!"

"I can beat that," Ricky tells me. "Back in the 1940s, a computer was as big as a school bus!"

20TH CENTURY LIFE
BOOK 5: THE 1940s

THE BIG FAT BOOK OF HISTORY

The Amazing
X-ray
Shoefitter!

SWELL SLANG FROM
THE 1940s!
Brown cow: chocolate milk
Cut a rug: to dance
Dish: a pretty girl
Dough: money
Duck soup: easy
Mothball: a serious student
Nervous pudding: Jell-O
Pancake turner: a DJ
Put on the dog: to dress and
act fancy
Take a powder: to leave

"Check out this old slang," I say. "If you studied all the time, other kids called you a mothball."

We both giggle.

1945 Computer: Five Tons of Fun

Out of milk? No need to go to the grocery store! In the 1940s, milkmen delivered bottles of fresh milk right to people's doorsteps.

Need to see a doctor? Just stay right in bed! In the 1940s, doctors came to patients' homes to lower fevers, cure the sniffles, and even deliver babies!

MAP OF THE 48 UNITED STATES OF AMERICA

Maps are sources that show us how the world has changed. A new town, state, or country means it's time for a new map!

I'm having so much fun, I almost forget what I'm looking for. Then— *jackpot!* I find a book with a whole chapter about TV.

I show it to Ricky.

SURVEY SHOWS CHILDREN SKIP HOMEWORK TO WATCH TV

Shocking headlines made the news in 1950. Kids would rather watch TV than do their homework! Luckily, they couldn't watch it all the time. The networks only broadcast shows late in the day. The rest of the time, if you turned on the TV, the screen looked the way it does on page 31.

30

31

"Guess kids really didn't watch TV in the afternoon," Ricky says. "Score another point for your grandpa."

"Okay," I say. "But he did forget to mention that they *couldn't* watch TV because there was nothing on!"

"Aren't you guys coming to lunch?" asks Anna.

I didn't even hear the bell. "Sure," I tell her. "Maybe we can get a brown cow."

"Or some nervous pudding," Ricky says.

Anna stares at us. "Some *what?*"

We tell her that's 1940s slang for chocolate milk and Jell-O.

Comparing lots of different sources will help you find the best information.

23

Ricky and I run straight to his grandma's house after school.

"Follow me," she says, and we go upstairs.

"Stand back, kids." She pulls a cord, and a ladder unfolds from a trapdoor in the ceiling!

"Is it hard to climb up there?" I ask.
Mrs. Vega grins. "Duck soup!"
I get it. She means it's *easy*.

The attic is piled up with old stuff. "I bet the last time anybody was here, the dinosaurs were still alive," Ricky jokes.

There are stacks of magazines. One has a photo of teenagers doing the jitterbug. I try to picture Grandpa Gus throwing Mrs. Vega up into the air and spinning her around. Yikes!

Want to find out what life was like at a certain time? Check out an old magazine. You'll see what people thought was cool, funny, scary, sad, and exciting.

Ricky picks up a comic. "Look! Superman!"
I didn't know they had Superman in the old days. There's Batman, too, and Wonder Woman!

"Ten cents?" Ricky exclaims. "I just paid three dollars for a Superman comic book!"

Five cents for an ice cream cone? Ten cents for a comic? Maybe Grandpa's twenty-five cents allowance wasn't so bad.

Artifacts are objects that tell us about the past. An artifact can be anything from an ancient tool to an old toy.

Back home, I go on the computer to see what else I can dig up about the old days.

"Okay if I come in?" Grandpa Gus asks.

"Sure," I say.

He looks at the screen.

"Well, what do you know? I had a baseball glove just like that," he says. "Saved for months to buy it. Cost me five dollars." Grandpa sighs. "Everything was cheaper back then."

"I know," I tell him.

"Too bad I'm not a kid in the old days," I say. "My allowance would buy a whole lot!"

SWELL BIKE
FOR GIRLS!
ONLY $30!

Grandpa laughs. "Times sure have changed. Tell you what. How would you like a job?"

"A job? What kind of job?" I ask.

"A job teaching me how to use the computer. And I'll pay you—at today's prices."

"Deal!" I say.

HIT SONGS OF THE '40s!
• All I Want for Christmas is My Two Front Teeth
• Bumble Boogie
• Zip A Dee Doo Dah

"Why were you looking all this up, anyway? Something for school?" Grandpa asks.

"Not exactly. I wanted to prove your stories weren't true. But I proved that they were."

"Checking up on your grandpa? Why, when I was your age—"

I wait for him to tell me about the old days.

"I would have done the same thing!" he says.

"Now, how about that job?" Grandpa smiles. "Do you think I can handle this contraption?"

"It's duck soup, Grandpa Gus. You'll learn in no time. Then you can buy a computer, and we can e-mail each other!"

It's funny. Times really *have* changed.
Grandpa used to teach me, and now *I'm*
teaching him!

Hi, Grandpa!
  Here I am making
strawberry jam—just
like you showed me!
  What are you
doing?
Love, Jamie

MAKING CONNECTIONS

Want to hear a good story? It's called *"history!"*

We discover the truth about history by studying different sources. A street sign, a birth certificate, yesterday's newspaper, a fifty-year-old magazine, a book from hundreds of years ago, and even an ancient cave painting all give us information that can unlock the secrets of the past. Sources are *everywhere.* Want to help solve the *mystery of history?* Just take a look around!

Look Back

- What does Grandpa Gus say about the snow on page 11? On page 14, what does Jamie learn from Mrs. Vega? On pages 15, 16, and 18, what sources prove Grandpa Gus's story?
- Look at pages 19 and 25. Where do Jamie and Ricky find more information?
- Look at the illustrations on pages 25 and 26. How many artifacts and sources can you spot?

Try This!

Blast from the Past! Find out more about the old days by interviewing a grandparent or an older neighbor or friend. Here are some starter questions:

- What was your school like?
- What were your favorite games, books, and movies?
- What did you do for fun in the summer?
- What was the best present you ever got?
- What things do kids have now that didn't exist when you were young?

    Bonus: Make your very own primary source by recording the interview.